Herman's Letter

TOM PERCIVAL

D0495440

Lancashire Library Services

30118128074477

PETERS	JF
£6.99	15-Nov-2013

Bloomsbury Publishing. London, New Delhi, New York and Sydney

First published in Great Britain in 2013 by Bloomsbury Publishing Plc
50 Bedford Square, London, WC1B 3DP

Text & illustrations copyright © Tom Percival 2013

The moral right of the author/illustrator has been asserted

All rights reserved
No part of this publication may be reproduced or transmitted
by any means, electronic, mechanical, photocopying or otherwise,
without the prior permission of the publisher

A CIP catalogue record for this book is available from the British Library

ISBN 978 1 4088 3674 3 (HB)
ISBN 978 1 4088 3675 0 (PB)

Printed in China by C & C Offset Printing Co Ltd,
Shenzhen, Guangdong

1 3 5 7 9 10 8 6 4 2

www.bloomsbury.com

For Daisy and Leila

Herman's Letter

TOM PERCIVAL

BLOOMSBURY

LONDON NEW DELHI NEW YORK SYDNEY

Herman and Henry had been best friends for as long as anyone could remember.

From tiddlywinks to climbing trees, they did everything together.

They had great fun inventing their own games and they even had
a secret club with a secret code and a TOP SECRET handshake.

Everything was just **perfect**...

It just wasn't fair!
Henry was off making new friends
while Herman was left on his own.

Herman Bear,
Herman's Hut,
The Wintery Woods,
Far Away.

HB6 4WW

Herman Bear,
Herman's Hut,
The Wintery Woods,
Far Away.

HB6 4WW

Herman had **meant** to write back
but how could he possibly
tell Henry how miserable he was?

So hours, days and months passed by and it was nearly time for Herman to hibernate.

He settled down in his comfiest armchair, pulled up a blanket and was just about to close his eyes when - WHUMPH!
- something clattered through the letterbox.
It was a letter! A letter from his best friend!

Herman Bear,
Herman's Hut,
The Wintery Woods,
Far Away.

HB6 4WW

Herman had never felt so happy. Henry missed him too!
He wrote a reply and rushed out through the snow to post it.

But he was too late.
The post office was shut for winter.
Herman groaned. What was he going to do?

Then he had a brilliant and rather bold idea.
He would deliver the letter himself!

Herman packed a suitcase and set out into the swirling snow.
He walked and walked and walked,
until his cosy home was just a distant memory.

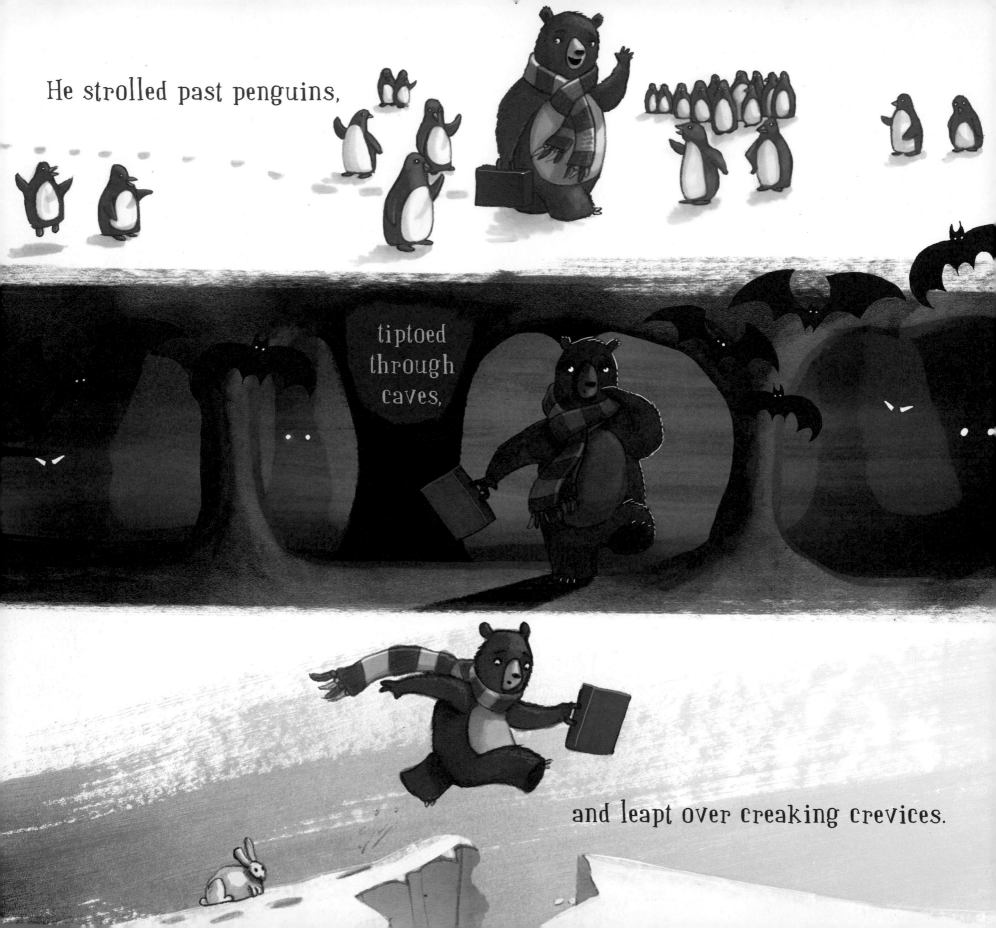

He strolled past penguins, tiptoed through caves, and leapt over creaking crevices.

Then he climbed

and climbed

and climbed –

up steep cliffs

and frozen

waterfalls –

until finally...

SCRAAAAPE!!!!

SCREE EE ECH!!!

He reached the top of the tallest
mountain he had ever seen.

Poor Herman! His journey
had just gone from bad to worse.

Oh bother.

Luckily, Herman was a very
resourceful bear.

But sometimes things don't go according to plan.

Herman bashed his head on a tree trunk and everything went...

BLAC

Herman's snoring attracted a lot of attention but nobody knew quite what to do.

Then somebody noticed
Herman's letter.

It was obvious. What they needed was a postman!

Later that afternoon, Henry was very surprised to receive a strange, snoring box. He was even more surprised when he opened it!

Henry Raccoon,
The New House,
The Big City,
Far Away.

HR7 8BC

Henry read Herman's letter and chuckled.

He didn't mind Herman dropping in unannounced –
after all, they were best friends…

But he had forgotten just how **loud** Herman's snoring was.

Suddenly spring seemed like
a very, very long way away...

RRRRRRRING!!!!

But when it did come,
it was BRILLIANT!